ZOMBIE
KONG

Novella

BOOKS of the DEAD

This book is a work of fiction. All characters, events, dialog, and situations in this book are fictitious and any resemblance to real people or events is purely coincidental.

Zombie Kong
Novella

Copyright 2012 by James Roy Daley

Cover art by Daniele Serra
Graphic design by Derek Daley
Interior design by James Roy Daley
Edited by Ashley Davis

FIRST EDITION

For more information check out:
BOOKSoftheDEADPRESS.com

For direct sales and inquiries contact:
besthorror@gmail.com

1 2 3 4 5 6 7 8 9 10

BOOKS of the DEAD

Dr. Steven Rutgers
UNDERSTANDING
ZOMBIE KONG

The average size of a small intestine in an adult human male is approximately twenty-three feet long and three centimeters wide. It's not uncommon for an intestine to reach a length of about thirty feet if the person is considered obese. Once a person dies that same intestine can measure up to 50% longer due to the loss of muscle tone within the tissue. With such losses, a three hundred pound man that has been dead for a few days can have a small intestine reaching a length of approximately forty-five feet. A three hundred pound gorilla that has been dead for the same amount of time will have a small intestine that is similar in both width and length.

The average height of a male silverback gorilla is 1.7 meters, or about 5' 7". A gorilla at this height typically has a weight of approximately 390 pounds, or 5.82 pounds per linear inch. Most experts agree that the gorilla, now referred to as "Zombie Kong," was slightly more than 52 feet tall and had a weight nearing 20 tons (40,000 pounds), or 64 pounds per linear inch. I have tried to find some facts and figures regarding the actual pre-death anatomy of the great beast but so far I have been unsuccessful. It should be noted that my own investigations have led me to believe that Zombie Kong's small intestine was close to 30cms in diameter and more than 400 feet long. 400 feet, for reference sake, is roughly 14% longer than the soccer field inside Wembley Stadium.

Zombie

Kong

James Roy Daley

ZOMBIE KONG

DALE

When the giant zombie gorilla tossed me into his mouth he did not chew, nor did he swallow. Instead, he turned his head and roared. The sound, quite simply, was the loudest thing I had ever heard.

Hugging the monster's dehydrated tongue while balancing on one knee, I found myself desperate and highly troubled. The massive teeth stacked around me were frightful. The canines interposing the calcified walls resembled the grand ivory tusks found on an African elephant, only thicker, more dangerous, and somehow... sinister.

The animal's mouth sprang open and snapped shut. Then it opened again, slowly this time, allowing sunlight to creep in like the promise of a morning that would never come.

Trapped inside, clutching where I was able, in my state of absolute fear, I recognized those teeth as being something I had been extremely lucky to avoid. But how much longer could my good fortune continue? Another minute... maybe two? Clinging to that terrible wad of dead meat, which was cold and slimy and reeking so bad my eyes watered, my thoughts, when fully formed, were at best, unsystematically erratic. But I did manage to keep my wits. Oh yes. Somehow I managed that much. Just.

While smudging the dirty tears across my face I looked past the monster's tongue, lips, and teeth, eying the world I thought I knew. But what kind of world was this? A flaming bus held no spectators. A squashed taxicab was overlooked. People running, a dog barking, fires consuming buildings that had been knocked over like mounds of blocks in a child's play-room.

There were cars—

Cars had been recklessly hurled across the land-scape and could be found leaning against trampled trees, which were snapped into sections, lying along-side busted telephone poles while live wires danced beside them. Dead bodies were scattered about, some-times in pieces, sometimes not. And for a moment— one *final* moment, I could only assume—I saw my wife Candice and my son Jake. Running. Screaming. Hand in hand, they were fleeing the monster inside a group of ten, one being a man I knew quite well: Roy Berkley.

Roy had dark hair, a slim nose, and a big smile wait-ing for me every time I saw him working at my local coffee shop. He always seemed to have everything in order. *Everything in its place,* he would sometimes say, smiling like a guy that had the whole world figured out. But if there's one thing I've learned in my life it's that while some men wear their hearts on their sleeves, others hide themselves behind a false exterior of coun-terfeit cheerfulness. I'd always assumed Roy to be a false exterior man, because his sleeves seemed to be whistle clean at all times… until that moment. Missing a limb and bleeding profusely, Roy fell to his knees with his mutilated arm flapping insanely, while the other pinwheeled for balance. With death but a wink from declaring the man I saw the look of terror fastened to his colorless face. A face haunted with fright. There was no false exterior at that moment. No sir. Everything was real. His feelings were genuine. Roy, I realized then, wore his heart on his sleeve. I almost felt bad for not knowing.

After Roy tumbled to the ground my wife looked over her shoulder, glancing at my friend before staring up at the animal... and straight at me. For a single moment, a *precious* moment, I like to think our eyes locked together, uniting our souls one last time before the oversized mouth closed tight, imprisoning me. Did it happen? Did we share a glance, or was my mind so lost within the depths of despair that I imagined the event? The answer remains unknown, for the moment the jaws closed my existence changed. The beast had me. And it swallowed me down. Whole.

I slipped past the pharynx, past the epiglottis and the larynx and into the tight confines of the esophagus. Before it happened I was wondering if I could free myself, for escaping my frightful predicament was the only option I was willing to entertain. But as the swallowing occurred and my world turned dark the prospect of escape looked bleak and unrealistic, unless of course, I could crawl my way back into that miserable mouth once again. It would be no easy task, and even if I managed to claw my way into that cursed place a second time, what then? What would I do? It was a practical question without a reasonable answer, but it didn't matter. If I couldn't re-enter the mouth I still had to escape. Somehow. Even if the esophagus muscles had already begun squeezing me, gripping me, pulling me down. Pulling me *in*.

I felt movement all around. I could tell by the way my world was shaking that the beast was walking, or perhaps running, for I was being pushed this way and that—shuffled about as if living through an earthquake.

Inside that moment, if I could feel grateful about one thing, it would be fact that the beast had swallowed me feet first. This isn't much to smile about, I know. But with my head pointing north and my feet pointing south I felt as if I had maintained *some* measure of control, as negligible as that control may seem.

Being inside an esophagus, which is a strange miracle of evolution, is like being devoured by a toothless python. It grips and pulls, squeezes and clutches, constricts and suffocates.

Suffocation. That was my newest fear, the latest thought picking at my brain and making my heart race, encouraging the sweat to bead up on my forehead and run squiggly trails down the back of my neck. But there *was* air inside the beast. Enough to breath, anyhow. There wasn't as much as I wanted, but there was more than I could have hoped for considering the situation.

Grunting and cursing, I dug my fingers into a wall of flesh. A handful of slippery, fungus-covered meat was my reward.

Something shifted and something moved beneath me. I heard a grunt and I lost my footing. The muscles in my body instinctively flexed as I tried to maintain my ground. I was leaving the esophagus. About to be dropped into that stretchy sack known as the stomach.

Gross.

Looking back, *that's* the first word that comes to mind. Not scary. Not terrifying. Not even murky or stinky... and it *was* stinky, *exceptionally* stinky. But as *rancid*, and *curdling*, and god-awful *barf-doggish* as it smelled, *gross* is the appropriate word.

Gross, man.

When I dropped out of the esophagus and into the stomach it was *gross*. It was also dark; I could hardly catch a glimpse of anything. There *was* air… sort of, which is why I didn't die. But the air was *so* wrong. The taste on my lips was akin to bile.

I should point out that there were holes in the stomach, the skin, and the muscles of the abdominal area. Every few seconds the beast would twist one way or another and a little bit of light would seep into the sack, and with light came nitrogen and oxygen and all the other molecules of gobbledygook that we call air.

By the way, do you know what a stomach is?

I know you're well aware that you *have* a stomach, but do you know what a stomach is? I mean, *really* know?

Let me tell you:

A stomach is a mixer wrought like a J-shaped bag. It churns, mashes, and pulverizes all the food that travels down the esophagus, slamming it together and breaking it into small pieces of fodder. This is done with the help of stomach muscles and the gastric juices that the walls of the stomach create.

And there I was—hanging out in a stomach, waiting to get broken down into digestible fragments of pulverized fodder. But there was a snag. The beast no longer *had* gastric juices. After the beast died the juices went missing.

My guess—and this *is* a guess—is that the enzymes and acids that aid with food digestion had leaked out, or dried up, or eaten their way through the tissue. No stomach acid meant *no digesting*. Fantastic news, for sure… however, I found myself sitting in something terrible, something snaking around in a slow moving in a circle.

A question came; it was simple and obvious.

What am I going to do?

The answer…

Phone my wife.

A stupid solution, I know. But it was all I had.

I suppose now, looking back at the situation, I could have called 911. The thought never occurred to me. So I rammed my hand into my front pocket and pulled out my cell phone, thinking about Candice. My keys—house keys, car keys, garage keys, a couple of mystery keys—they also came out of my pocket and they slipped from my fingers. The keys were gone, but I still had my phone and that was the important thing.

I looked to my left. No keys in sight.

I looked to my right, just as the monster released another roar, and this time the noise was louder than I can possibly explain. The sound was coming from everywhere, all directions. The sound was penetrating, getting right inside me, into my heart. When the noise ended I found that I was screaming in terror with a hand gripping my chin and my bottom lip trembling uncontrollably. Frightened beyond words, I clicked on my phone and coughed a number of times, in desperate need of a germ-free environment.

The air, of course, *was* toxic. How long would it be before the air itself killed me? It was impossible to say, although I couldn't image I'd survive much longer.

I guess this is a good time to tell you I have asthma, for it was at that moment I felt the first signs of an asthma attack, which, in so many ways, was the very last thing I wanted to add to the situation.

Half the phone number was dialed with jittery hands; then I saw something and needed a moment to see it again. I hung up.

My phone, like most, came with a backlight. And because I had a light I could see…

Dead bodies.

I was sitting in a pile of dead bodies: faces pale, mouths opened, noses smashed, eyes locked in fear, arms chewed into mulch, scalps yanked from heads, skin torn, spines protruding from shattered backs, legs broken, fingers missing, feet twisted, kneecaps obliterated, a child…

A child with little yellow ribbons braided into her blonde hair… she had her face pounded into her shoulder. I saw a man that had been bitten in half at the waist; he looked about forty. A pair of chubby arms sat alone, stacked together almost neatly on a mangled corpse. The owner of the arms was nowhere to be found.

I saw a baseball glove, an unopened bottle of wine, a laptop, a pack of cigarettes, a pair of sunglasses, and what I later realized was a horse's head, covered in blood, guts, and bone. And this—*all this*—was turning in a circle, blending, mixing, churning.

Fighting for balance, I stood up and dialed my wife's number. My legs sank into the mulch.

And then it had me: the small intestine. I was going in.

The phone began ringing.

Candice answered, sounding completely stressed out. "Hello?"

"Hello?"

"Dale, is that you?"

"Oh my God, yes! It's me! It's me!"

"Where are you? I thought—"

"I'm inside the monkey!"

A slight pause came before Candice said, "What?!"

"I'm inside! He tossed me into his mouth and swallowed me down!"

"You're kidd—"

Panic consumed me in a way I can't possibly explain, and I started screaming: "I'M IN THE MONKEY'S STOMACH! YOU'VE GOT TO TELL SOMEBODY! HELP ME! GET ME THE HELL OUT OF HERE! I'VE GOT TO GET—"

The monster unleashed another thought-crushing yell and pounded on his chest. Instead of finishing the sentence I screamed more loudly than before. Then something happened. Not inside. Outside. Maybe the monster fell; maybe he jumped off a car or did something as simple as sit down. I don't know, but my center of gravity changed and the corpses around me shifted position. The dead were piling my way, causing the phone to pop from my hand and tumble from my fingers. The world became a fraction darker than the far side of the moon and before I had a chance to catch my breath—before I realized what was about to happen—Kong's intestine sucked me in.

CANDICE

"Hello? Hello!?" Candice hung up and dialed her husband back at once. After several rings the answering service came on so she hung up and tried her luck again, only to be addressed with the same prerecorded greeting that had annoyed her the moment before.

As she hung up a second time her son Jake said, "What is it, Mommy? Was that Daddy? Is he okay?"

Candice looked her boy in the eye, smiling falsely. He was so young. So scared. "Everything's fine, Jake." she lied.

Everything wasn't fine. Nothing was fine.

"Was that Daddy?"

"Yes."

"Is he—"

"Jake, *please!*" Standing on the sidewalk next to a misshapen motorcycle, Candice exhaled a deep breath and placed her thumb between her teeth. It was something she often did when she was feeling nervous or upset. After tossing her cell phone into her purse she wrapped her purse-strap around her shoulder and crouched down like a rugby player in a huddle, eyes scoping the ground. One hand gripped her forehead while the other was planted on her knee. She thought she might faint. Or throw up. Or both.

She didn't mean to snap at Jake. Her only child deserved better than *that*, especially now. But the situation was a little too much to handle and she didn't know if she could take it. The summer heat was too much; it wasn't at all pleasurable. And there was a giant zombie gorilla smashing the town apart. Worse still, the man she married nine years ago—on a spring day filled with rain and hail and 75 mile-an-hour winds that destroyed a tree and smashed a church window— was calling her on a telephone from inside the animal's stomach. This was a *colossal* situation. And yeah… she could admit it: she was worried, she was scared; she was freaking right the fuck out.

"Jake."

"Yes Mom?"

"I'm freaking out."

"What?"

"Sorry, I'm… I'm having a hard time with this."

Jake didn't say anything. He just stood there, looking at his mother with concern rooting its way into his features. He was trying to be a big boy, trying not to cry, but his mother had never looked so worried. So upset. So saddened. Never. Not once. Not even on the day that Aunt Margie died. That was a bad day but *this* was worse. *Way* worse. He wasn't having *any* fun— none whatsoever. Nothing here was making him happy, and it was a *Saturday*. Weekends were supposed to be nothing *but* fun, not like this. Not scary.

At once Candice stood tall. She snatched Jake's hand and started walking. Together they marched along the sidewalk and onto the road, ignoring the sirens blaring, the people weeping, and the dead bodies littering the area around them. They walked past a woman that had fallen to her knees and a man that was openly crying. They moved their way through a cloud of smoke and past a blue pick-up truck that had a huge dent in the hood. The dent seemed to be full of implication, much like the flat tires, the broken windshield, and the young man strapped into his seat, impaled with glass.

Candice tugged on Jake's hand, encouraging the boy to turn his head away from the truck. She didn't want him to observe such a catastrophe, even though tragedy could be easily witnessed from every direction.

They kept walking.

Jake could see that his mother was taking him into a greasy spoon that had a faded billboard attached to a brick wall above a dirty strip of windows. The billboard had the words—

-THE LUNCH ROOM-
Putting smiles of faces since 1968!

—stenciled across its front.

Candice pulled the door open and trudged past a *PLEASE WAIT TO BE SEATED* notice with Jake in hand. They moved down an aisle that had a row of vacant booths on each side and sat next to a window, facing each other in an empty cubicle that had nothing cluttering the table.

She opened her purse, pulled out her phone, and made her call again. Nothing.

Broken dishes peppered the floor. Half-eaten meals sat abandoned on tables gathering flies. Someone had left a purse sitting in the booth next to them, along with an iPod and a pair of cheap sunglasses. On a different table a twenty-dollar bill, folded in the middle, had been tossed atop an empty plate. There were no waitresses to be found, no cooks, or hungry customers, or people standing behind the counter eager to serve food. Aside from Jake and Candice there was only one other person in the restaurant: a stiff-jointed man with a chiseled face and razor short hair. He might have been thirty-five years old, give or take a year.

Standing motionlessly in the center of the room, beneath a ceiling fan that spun wobbly-circles above him, the man looked a little bit like a shorthaired version of Jack Nicholson back in the 1970s. Specifically, when Jack played the role of Randle Patrick McMurphy in the film *One Flew Over the Cuckoo's Nest,* except the man in the restaurant wasn't wearing a white hospital shirt; he was wearing a referee's jersey, covered in dust. And he didn't seem cheerfully zealous. He seemed downright weird.

It took Candice a moment to remember the sports store across the street and grasp the fact that the people working there wore the referee jersey as part of their uniform. The store, *Athlete's Delight,* had always done excellent business as far as she could tell. She had assumed it always would. Of course, that was before—

Slowly, as if he was in a trance, the man cocked his head towards them. He looked at Jake. Then Candice. "What do we have here?" he said.

Technically it was a question, but he wasn't asking it to anyone in particular. He just said it—quietly, almost emotionlessly, with his eyes locked on the empty space between them. He mumbled something under his breath after speaking, and then he stumbled forward. In some ways he looked like he was suffering the effects of a voodoo curse.

A moment of silence came, followed by Jake leaning across the table, whispering, "That man's acting funny, Mom. Look at him. Look at his hands. Do you see what he's doing with his hands?"

Candice looked over her shoulder. Once again her thumb found its way between her teeth.

Meaner than a pit-bull with blood on its snout, the man was opening his hands slowly then snapping them into fists, then opening them once again, and snapping them into fists—repeating the motion, over and over. If the oddball look sheet-rocked across his vacuous face wasn't reason for concern, the way he was moving his hands definitely was. The guy had toys in the attic; it wouldn't have surprised Candice if he pulled his pants to his knees and sang Happy Birthday in French while doing a jig.

"Mom," Jake said. "Do you think—"

"Quiet. Don't look at him. Just… ignore him for now."

"But—"

"Hush!"

Jake nodded and his eyes found the table but felt no comfort knowing his mother was ignoring something that needed to be addressed. The smell of lunacy was in the air, only she didn't recognize it, or perhaps she didn't care. He wanted to tell her that the man was not in touch with things, only he could not find the words.

Candice considered leaving the restaurant but needed a moment to think, and the relative tranquilly of room was the most she could hope for.

Help. She needed help. And she needed to do something smart, but what? What could she do? Her husband Dale had phoned her from inside the gorilla's belly and he wanted her to do *WHAT* exactly? What was she supposed to do about *this* little situation, phone the police? Without a doubt, the police were already well aware of the fact that there was a giant gorilla smashing the shit out of the town, so that was one phone call she didn't have to make.

She needed a cigarette.

Or better yet, a joint… a big fat one. One grown by Snoop Dogg, rolled by Ziggy Marley, and endorsed by Cheech and his good buddy Chong.

"Oh God," she muttered. "I don't know what to do about this."

She looked out the window.

On the far side of the street most of the buildings had been knocked down. *Athlete's Delight*, she realized, had been replaced with a pile of rubble that had a flattened car squashed into it.

The man spoke again: "What do we have here? Who do you think you are?"

Candice found herself wishing there was a waitress in the house so she could order a cup of coffee and look at the menu. She turned towards the counter. As luck would have it a pot of Joe was sitting right there, looked like it had been freshly brewed, too. She turned towards Jake. "Would you like something to drink? A chocolate milk, maybe? Coke?"

Jake nodded. "Okay, Mom."

"Which?"

"Huh?"

"Which? Coke?"

"Coke."

"Okay. I'll get you a—"

"No, wait. Chocolate milk. I want chocolate milk."

"Okay. Chocolate milk it is. Stay right here and I'll fetch us some drinks. Then we'll figure out what to do." Candice forced a smile.

Jake tried to do the same but failed.

After plunking her phone and her purse on the table, she stood up and started walking, avoiding the man standing the center of the restaurant. As she was making her way behind the counter she heard the man say, "What are you doing?"

She didn't respond.

His hands opened slowly and snapped shut.

She was getting a bad feeling, a scary feeling. A feeling of imminent doom.

Two modern-looking refrigerators with glass doors sat together like wide-shouldered soldiers. Inside the unit on the left there was an entire shelf dedicated to milk, chocolate milk, and cream.

She opened the appropriate door, reached inside, and liberated a liter of chocolate milk. The container had a cartoon drawn, brown-colored cow licking its lips with its eyebrows raised, suggesting the milk it produced was ten times more delicious than the milk from any other cow.

As she sat the carton on the counter the man spoke again. His eerie voice was enough to make her skin crawl: "You're not allowed back there. Get away from there!"

The man was suddenly coming at her with a noticeable amount of aggression in his awkward movement. His head was still cocked sideways in an outlandish predatory gesture, but more disturbing was his eyes. Chicken-eyes, red-rimmed, frightful and filled with the promise of pain; they were lit up like hateful firestorms.

Before Candice knew it would happen she snatched the container of milk from the counter and held it up defensively; it was a knee-jerk reaction, not a game plan. She found herself backing away while scanning the restaurant for a weapon more threatening than a cold beverage.

Within seconds the man was behind the counter with her, getting close, reaching for her milk.

God damn, what the hell was he trying to do?

"You're not allowed back here!" he announced. Lines materialized in his forehead as he slapped the container across the restaurant. The container soared, turning circles, leaving a splattering of bubbly chocolate in its wake.

Candice managed to say: "What—?" before his hands—both of them—wrapped around her neck.

He began choking her.

She backed into a corner, struggling to free herself. The bulk of her thoughts centered around a common theme: *Why are you doing this? Why would you do this? Why is this happening? Why do you want to hurt me? Why are you attacking me?*

Why, why, why?

Then a new thought came: *How can I make this stop?*

Overwhelmed, she looked towards the counter, searching for a weapon—a knife, preferably.

Her eyes widened.

There was a knife—two of them, in fact—but they were too far away to be useful. There was a spoon, however, and it was well within her grasp.

She reached her hand out and her fingers tickled the spoon's long handle. As her fingers were making contact with the would-be weapon the man shook her violently and the entire world seemed to fade out of focus. The man's hard looking face and undersized eyes grew faint. The room darkened. The air thinned. She would soon pass out.

The man said, "Did you see what happened? You should have done something! I know you! You're the reason things are like this!"

"I don't—"

There was a scream—

Jake was screaming, standing on the other side of the counter with his eyes the size of beer coasters and his mouth wide open.

Beyond the screams Candice could hear the clatter of gunfire mingled with the sound of the beast's roar. Little stars began appearing in the darkness of her eyes. Jake's words of protest shrank into mumbles. Her body felt weak, worse than the moment before. She wanted to tell Jake to get away from the man, not to worry about the gunfire or the monster on the street. She wanted to tell him that things would be okay. But things might *not* be okay. What would happen to Jake if the man successfully choked her to death? And... was that his objective? Did he plan on killing her because of the things that were happening outside, or stranger yet, over a glass of chocolate milk? Really? Why would anyone want to do a thing like that? Comprehending the situation was like trying to inhale a baseball.

The knife. She needed the knife.

Wrong.

There were two knives, neither one close enough to grab. What was that other thing she was trying to snag from the counter, a fork?

No... a *spoon*. A long-handled spoon.

She whacked the counter with the palm of her hand and shifted her body's weight. The man tumbled back a step and for a moment his grip weakened. Then his teeth pressed together and his face seemed to age a dozen years. He was squeezing hard now, as if he was trying to make her head pop from her neck.

Candice wrapped her fingers around the oval end of the spoon and lifted it from the counter. She had it. She had a weapon. The handle end of the spoon seemed like the world's dullest blade but that was okay. It wasn't meant for carving a Christmas turkey at the White House; it was meant for serving up a big old pile of whoop-ass right here in The Lunch Room.

Putting smiles of faces since 1968!

As she lifted the weapon she noticed the man's nametag. It said: KIRBY.

A muffled grunt came. She thought—*Well Kirby... I've got a little somethin' for ya*—and a second later she slammed the spoon into the man's face, just below his temple. She could only assume it passed through his nasal cavity, and bone, and whatever muscles were in that general area.

The man fell away from her—stumbling, tripping, staggering like a drunken barfly at closing time. Mouth opening and closing, nose running; his eyes glossed over. And with that came the screams, and the blood, and a look that was one part shock, one part terror, and three parts pain.

Coughing. Coughing. Candice was free of his grip and coughing... but she was breathing again and not a moment too soon. With less than an athlete's agility she snailed her way over the counter, took Jake by the hand, and made for the door.

"You corpse-fucker!" Kirby managed to shriek, pivoting towards her with blood parading down his face. His hands clenched together... again, and again. His fingernails were biting his palms.

Once Candice and Jake were outside they felt the ground shake beneath them, as if a miniature earthquake was taking place.

It was no earthquake, they soon realized. But it was *something.*

Something big.

Candice saw it first: Zombie Kong.

The monster was less than ten feet away.

And looking directly at the boy.

DALE

Once I was inside the small intestine I thought I was going to die.

If you can imagine yourself wrapped head-to-toe in cold, rancid, deli-meat, you might be able to comprehend that moment of my life. Kong's intestine was clinging to my body like a wetsuit made of liver. There was no free space—none, aside from a little bit of room around my neck.

I opened my mouth—perhaps to scream, perhaps to breath... I honestly don't know—and that's when chunks of wet slop pushed onto my tongue.

In a desperate attempt to eject the foul tasting filth I coughed and spat, but every moment my mouth was open, things became worse for me. My mouth was becoming packed full. My nose was too. With my elbows bent, I pushed my hands away from my chest, trying to create a pocket of freedom. It wasn't working. I began to swallow, and suffocate. I realized that I was *being* eaten; I *had been* eaten. The fact that I was still alive was nothing short of a miracle, and if things didn't soon change I would pay the ultimate price.

Which is one of the reasons I believe God was with me that day.

Growing up, I never believed in God. But now I do.

God is the resurrection; He brings us eternal life.

You see, as I was pushing my hands away from my body I felt a hard object touching my fingers, and before I had a chance to comprehend what the object was, I found myself reunited with my keys.

Blunt as they were, I decided to cut myself free.

Freedom, it seemed, was in the palm of my hand.

Jesus, as it is so often said, saves.

KIRBY

The gunfire and the screaming mingled with the sound of a siren blaring. The woman had turned her head away from the sharpest of the sounds before latching onto the boy's hand and rushing down the street, through the dust and the smoke, away from Zombie Kong, dragging the child along at a speed that could not be comfortable for either of them. In return Zombie Kong pounded both fists against his chest, raised his head away from his lumbering shoulders, and roared. His left hand swung wide, inadvertently swatting the restaurant with his knuckles, causing the walls to shake and the large windows near the front door to shatter. Glass collapsed to the floor and sprayed inside the building, some landing near Kirby's feet as the monster trudged away.

Kirby dismissed the broken glass and the chaos on the street, for his thoughts were elsewhere: on the *bitch* that *stabbed* him!

Carefully, delicately, he took hold of the spoon. Holding his breath in his throat he pulled the handle from his face. Once the task was completed he released the spoon, allowing it to fall to the floor by his feet. Touching the fresh wound with shaky fingers, smudging a line of sweaty blood along his tender skin; a gasp escaped. His nose began bleeding and tears rolled from his eyes.

That corpse-fucker, he thought. *That dry-cunt-slut is going to die.*

How do you like those tomatoes?

Looking towards the broken window Kirby paused. Then he began to laugh, but it was a cold laugh, void of happiness, almost emotionless in its tone.

Tonight the world would fear Zombie Kong but tonight that *BITCH* would fear *him!*

He walked towards the table the bitch-woman and the boy had occupied. He picked up the bitch's phone, which had been left unguarded. He squeezed it like he hated it and flung it across the room before picking up her purse. Looking inside he found her keys and her wallet. Inside her wallet he found her driver's license, which let him know that the bitch-woman had a name: Candice Wanglund. Apparently Candice lived at 726 Mower Street, a mere three blocks away.

Oh, this was good. He had been waiting for years to deliver a little payback for all those times he had been lied to, and laughed at, and picked on. Ever since the third grade bitches like Candice had been getting the best of him, making him feel stupid, making him feel like an outcast. Only back then they weren't bitch-women, they were bitch-girls—bitch-girls that grew up to be bitches… like Candice… the bitch. He was sick of it. If only they knew now nice he could be, how sweet, how Goddamn pleasant. But bitch-women like this Candice cunt never want to see the good side of people; they only want to see the bad. They only wanted to push you down, point fingers at you, treat you like a second-class citizen. Bitches only want to hurt people. Nice people. Nice people like him.

No more.

It was time to take a stand.

The time for resolution was today.

Stepping outside with the bitch's keys and identification snug in his pocket, another building crumbled to the ground, unloading a fresh cloud of dust and debris across what was quickly becoming a wasteland.

Looking left he could see several policemen firing at the giant beast while another officer, standing alone among the dead, loaded his weapon. Looking right he watched the path of destruction continue. Cars were being flipped over. Telephone poles were being smashed apart. The monster was on the move.

And there she was, the bitch-woman: Candice Wanglund, running down the street without a care in the world.

Who did she think she was?

What gave her the right?

Hands opening slowly before snapping into fists, Kirby followed. With blood flowing down his face and a feverish sweat escaping from his pores, thoughts of committing murder were overwhelming, making residence in the forefront of his mind.

CANDICE

Guns were firing and people were screaming. There was a giant blaze in the center of the road. Zombie Kong was close to the blaze, trotting along the asphalt, snarling and angry and searching for another mouth-sized meal. The ugliness of his face was absolute.

Candice needed a safe place; that much was obvious. But where?

Without giving it much thought she made her way past a burning car and towards a three-story apartment building on the far side of the road. It was an older structure; one that was built in the 1920s and had time-weathered gargoyles perched on the rooftop. It didn't occur to her until she was on the doorstep that the heavy-looking door might be locked. Thankfully it wasn't. With a shove and a grunt she was inside, pulling Jake to the center of a gloomy foyer where there was no elevator in sight, only a couple of mystery doors and a dingy staircase that had been walked on a hundred million times.

Upstairs or down?

She began making for the basement before the image of Zombie Kong knocking over the building, burying her alive in the rubble, came crashing in.

She didn't want to be in the basement.

Upstairs was a better bet so up they went, all the way to the third floor. After jostling their way through a grimy access door they entered a hallway that was in hopeless need of modern light fixtures and a fresh coat of paint. The run-down building seemed eerily quiet, too quiet, as if—

Pause. "Hello?"

Nothing.

"Hello? We need help!" Candice rapped her knuckles against a door marked 302. Without waiting she tried her luck with 301 and 303, which were beside each other on the opposite side of the hall.

"Where is everyone?" Jake asked.

"Gone. I bet everyone in the building was evacuated as soon the town became a war zone."

"What are we going to do?"

Candice's eyes narrowed. She placed her hand on the nearest doorknob and discovered the door to be unlocked. Pushing it wide, she whispered, "Hello? Anybody home?"

No response.

A shrug.

They stepped inside and Jake closed the door. "How did you know the door would open?" he asked.

"I didn't."

"Oh."

The sounds of the battle on the street were frighteningly loud. The apartment wasn't safe. It was, however, small and unpredictably pleasant. A widescreen television was attached to a wall across from a stylish couch. The original hardwood floors had been sanded and stained a warm brown color. There was a laptop computer and a printer sitting on a beautiful oak desk, next to a small wine rack that was 90% stocked. In the left hand corner of the room an old but gorgeous bow window allowed a great deal of light to shine throughout the space.

Candice was surprised.

Jake might not have noticed that the residence was too nice for the apartment, but she did. She couldn't help wondering why someone would leave a home un-locked inside of a rundown building if they owned such nice things. But then she looked out the window, and figured people had left in a hurry. Her new per-spective offered a clear view of the area around her, both east and south. What she saw was terrifying.

The town was destroyed.

Turning away, she said, "Jake, are you okay?"

"Yes. I'm okay."

"Great. I'm going to—"

There was a monstrous roar, loud enough to make her flinch. She spun around quickly and was taken back by her view of Zombie Kong. The great beast was standing in front of the window with its arms raised and fury dominating its pure white eyes. A huge trail of intestines littered the area beneath its feet, rop-ing their way from its midsection, along the creature's leg, to the road.

"Jake," Candice muttered, barely loud enough to distinguish. "Move away from the window. Quickly, move away."

Kong's arms came smashing down. Massive fists pounded the road, causing cracks to appear in the pavement. At the same moment Jake took one step back, but Candice did not. She couldn't. The pande-monium playing out before her was drawing her atten-tion like nothing else would. She could see policemen and townspeople alike, standing in the street, openly firing their weapons with a complete disregard for safety. It was clear they were determined to bring the monster to its knees, even if it meant sacrificing their own lives in the process.

The gunfire continued for another few seconds be-fore Candice was handed the shock of her life.

It was Dale! Her husband Dale—suspended in the air, hanging half-in and half-out of Kong's abdominal area with his arms flopping and his head bouncing in whichever direction gravity demanded it.

"Oh God," she whispered with her thumb at her teeth.

Dale was dead.

He *had* to be dead, didn't he?

Kong spun left and as a result Dale slipped free and fell to the ground, landing awkwardly in the mound of intestines.

The next pair of seconds seemed to last a lifetime while Candice grappled with the reality of the situation.

She forged a plan—a simple one, and a dangerous one.

Turning towards her son she said, "Jake, stay right here. I'll be back in a minute."

"What?" he said. "You're leaving?"

"I need to—"

"Mom, no! Don't go! Don't leave me!"

"Jake, I—"

"Mom!"

"Listen!"

"No! If you're going somewhere, let me come with you!"

Candice considered, and disregarded, her son's request. She stepped forward, grabbed Jake by the hand, and dragged him towards the window.

"Look!" she shouted. "Look! Do you see what that is? That's your father on the street and he needs help. I'm going out there to get him!"

Jake didn't know where he was supposed to look; his eyes were flicking from one thing to the next. "Where?"

"Right there! See?"

Dead bodies. Squashed cars. Weapons firing. People running. Smashed buildings. Smoke. Ash. Dust. Fire. Kong.

"I don't see—"

"There!"

Jake saw it.

At first he wasn't sure what he was looking at, but then he knew. His father was lying beneath Kong, a moment away from being stepped on and killed, if he wasn't dead already.

"Is that—? Are you sure?"

"That's your Dad, Jake. He's on the road, I'm going out there to save him, and you're staying right here. Don't... move... a muscle."

"But—"

"*But* nothing. I'm going, and you're not coming with me. It's too dangerous." Still holding Jake by the hand, she dragged him into the center of the room, away from he conflict. "Now listen to me, Jake. I don't want you to leave this apartment, not for any reason, you here?"

A reluctant nod of the head. "Yes."

"Okay?"

"Okay."

"Promise me."

"Mom, I promise. I won't go anywhere."

"And don't look out the window."

"What? Why not?"

"Stay away from the window, Jake. I mean it. The last thing we need is for the monster to notice you."

Jake's eyes shifted, and for a moment he was lost in thought. He said, "It *is* a monster, isn't it?"

She nodded, and admitted, "Yes, Jake. It is."

"You said monsters don't exist."

"I was wrong. Now stay here and behave. I'll be right back."

Without kissing her son goodbye, or giving him a hug, or telling him that she loved him, Candice made for the door. With so much on her mind she never thought twice about it. But Jake did. So while tears formed in the boy's eyes, Candice was running the length of the hallway and through the grimy access door. She flew past a fire extinguisher and down the stairs two at a time until she found herself in the front foyer. She slowed her pace as she approached the front door. After taking a deep breath she opened the door and slowly stepped outside.

The gunfire continued. Kong was standing in the center of the street, pounding his chest. He released a horrific roar and turned away.

Dale was still there, still lying among the intestines that littered the street. If she was going to save him, this was the time.

"On the count of three," she whispered. "One, two… three…"

She didn't move.

What the hell am I going to do? she questioned. *Just run out there and grab him?*

Yes. Just run out there and grab him, then drag him to safety.

That's crazy.

Of course it is.

I can't do it.

Yes you can.

Really?

Yes.

What if he's already dead?

Just do it. Do it. Dale needs you.

But…

Just go.

Go!

Kong, in a state of rage, pummeled a foot against the ground, missing Dale by less than two feet.

Suddenly Candice was running. And screaming.

Her plan was so friggin' stupid, so foolish! But there she was, racing towards the monster like an idiot, straight into the mouth of madness.

The gunfire stopped at once, as if every cop and wannabe trooper had been given the order. But that wasn't the case. The fact was, they could see her: the crazy woman that was trying to get herself killed. One voice shouted, "What is she doing?" Another voice announced, "Get away from there!" And Kong turned his head quickly, knowing something was happening.

Candice kept running. She didn't care.

She was less than twenty feet from Kong and getting closer by the second.

This was it. If she died, so be it. At least she would die trying to save the man she loved. Wasn't that an honorable thing to do? Wasn't that courageous? Dying like a hero was worth something, right?

Fifteen feet.

But what about Jake? What about the *boy* she loved? What would happen to her son if he lost his mother and his father both? What would he do? Who would take care of him?

Ten feet.

Candice realized that she didn't think things through.

Oh God, she thought. *I left Jake alone. I told him to wait for me. I told him not to move a muscle. What was I thinking? What have I done? What will happen to my boy if I don't survive this incredibly idiotic mission?*

I didn't even kiss him goodbye!

I didn't tell him that I love him!

Five Feet.

And I do love him! I love him more than anything! Oh shit! This is a mistake! What I'm doing right now is a mistake! A giant mistake! What will happen if Zombie Kong starts kicking the shit out of the apartment building?

What will Jake do?

Will he just stand there, and...

NOT... MOVE... A MUSCLE?

Damn!

Candice found herself tripping across huge intestines. Before she knew it would happen she was down on one knee, leaning over her husband with Kong standing above—roaring, snarling, and slamming a tight fist into an open hand.

"Dale!" Candice shouted. "Dale! Are you okay? Are you all right? Speak, damn you... speak!"

But Dale, covered in rancid smelling slime, wasn't speaking. He wasn't saying anything. He couldn't. He was either dead or unconscious.

Dead. Surely he's dead, she thought, when the world became quiet.

Too quiet. Yes... the sounds of a town gone mad were still there, but something was different. Something had changed.

Candice looked up.

And realized that Zombie Kong was looking down. Its eyes, huge and milky white, sat wide upon its face and heavy upon her, not following her, for she was not moving. She couldn't move. Fear had bonded her to the earth.

JAKE

"What are you doing here, child?"

Jake spun like a top, startled by the voice.

In his mind he had already come to the conclusion that whoever was asking the question would be someone terrible, someone that extracted a great deal of pleasure from torturing little boys that had been left alone in strange places, someone like that nasty fellow in the restaurant, the insane man that tried to kill his mother. Or perhaps it wasn't someone *like* the man from the restaurant; perhaps it *was* the man from the restaurant. Of course, the voice sounded different, very different. But what if it was a trick? Nasty-man could be tricky, he was sure of it.

It was no trick.

In the doorway was a woman he had never seen before, an attractive lady with dark skin and short dark hair. Her accent was Brazilian, not that Jake was able to place it. He couldn't. From the look of her she seemed more puzzled than angry, but that didn't mean she couldn't be terrible.

Terrible people could be disguised in pretty packages. He needn't look any further then Mary Hershel, the girl living across the street, to have proof of that. All the boys in the neighborhood seemed to think the sun and the moon inhabited the sky just to please her, but if her outsides could represent her insides, Jake figured Mary would look like an alligator.

"Are you alone?" the woman asked.

Stepping away uneasily, Jake said, "My mom will be back in a minute."

"Where is she?"

"We were trying to get away from the monster."

Confused, the woman asked, "Did I leave my door open?"

"It was unlocked. We weren't doing anything bad, we just needed a place to go." He doubted the woman would believe him. Adults never believed it when kids said everything was okay. They only seemed to believe kids when they were coming clean and admitting they did something wrong. Apparently that's what kids were best at: doing something wrong.

"So... your mom, where is she?"

Jake pointed towards the window. "Outside."

"She left you here?"

"Like I said, she'll be back in a minute." Jake felt salty tears forming in his eyes, followed by the ugly feeling of confused shame.

The woman walked towards the window quickly, leaving the door to the apartment wide open. Before she made it across the room she was taken back by her visuals. The gunfire had stopped, but Kong was in plain view.

She turned towards the boy. "This is no good."

Apologetically, Jake offered, "I'm sorry," feeling like he'd been caught with his hand in the cookie jar. "We didn't come into your place for any reason... other than needing a place to go. My mom... she'll be back in a minute. She'll tell you the same thing when she gets here." His eyes pleaded with her, begging her to understand. Because the last thing he needed was trouble. *More* trouble.

"I don't care about that. I'm just saying we shouldn't be here... at all. It isn't safe."

"Oh."

"What's your name?"

"Jake. Jake Wanglund."

"Jake, my name's Latina. I came back to grab some things. Then I'm leaving and so are you." She walked across the room to the oak desk and opened a drawer.

"But I can't. Mom says—"

"Yes you can."

"No—"

"This is *my* home, child. Not yours. That puts me in charge, so listen a second." She pulled a metal box from the desk drawer, sat it next to the computer, and opened it. Inside the box was fifty-odd dollars in loose change and more than two hundred in bills. She folded the bills in half, slid them into her back pocket, and closed the lid. "I was just at my sister's place. Her name's Tobi. She lives in this same building, on the first floor. But she lives on the other side of the building, away from that... that... thing."

"Mom says it's a monster."

"And your mom is right. It *is* a monster, and I'm sure your mom doesn't want you getting hurt." She lifted a sheet of paper from the printer and pulled a pencil from a cup. "What's your last name again?"

"Wanglund."

She wrote a quick note, pulled a roll of Scotch Tape from drawer, clipped off a piece, and fixed it to the paper. She walked across the room and stuck the note on the exterior side of the door. "When your mother comes for you she'll know where to find you, and she'll be happy about it, child. She'll be glad you're with an adult. Trust me. It's a little safer there."

Jake opened his mouth to complain, but decided not to. Maybe the woman wasn't too bad after all. "Well..."

"You'll like Tobi. She's nice... and she loves little kids."

Jake grinned, feeling a touch better.

Latina stepped into her bedroom and came out a few seconds later with a fractured smile and handful of items stuffed into a gym bag. "Lets go."

Jake nodded and said, "Okay." He didn't want to be alone anyhow.

CANDICE

Kong was milliseconds from snuffing out both Candice and Dale with a single fist when he was hit with an onslaught on gunfire. Looking up, towards his attackers, he unleashed a forceful growl that could be felt as much as it could be heard.

Candice, nearly jumping out of her shoes, shrieked. The shriek, smothered beneath the conversation between beast and bullets, was short lived. This was her time to move and she knew it. She slapped Dale across the face, screaming, "Wake up, Dale! Wake up!"

Dale didn't move.

He might have been dead.

Without considering her options, she wrapped hopeful arms around Dale's slippery chest and dragged him over the mound of rotten entrails, away from Kong.

She hauled him a little more than ten feet prior to hearing: "We've got 'em, lady! Move!"

Before she knew it would happen two men were pushing her away and taking hold of Dale.

The men started running, dragging Dale along. One mentioned how awful Dale looked, not trying to be purposefully mean, just stating the obvious.

It was at that moment that Candice felt the most fear. Up until then she was grasping at straws and hoping for the best. It was a suicide mission, if she wanted to be honest with herself. Her chances of survival were next to nothing, meaning, in some ways she had nothing to lose. *Oh, but that wasn't true. She had Jake to lose. Problem was: she hadn't realized it until it was too late.* Nonetheless, once the two men became involved and it looked like she was going to complete her task she had *everything* to lose. And the terrified feelings she was hiding so well began overpowering her, causing her to think, causing her to worry... causing her toe to catch on a slab of Kong's flesh.

She fell to the ground.

Gunfire.

Shouting.

The monstrous roar.

Blood. It was dripping from her mouth—

Candice was lying facedown with her knees scraped and her elbows throbbing, and suddenly *she* was the one being dragged. The ground skimmed along beneath her. Her arms felt like they might get pulled from their sockets. "I'm okay," she managed to say. "I'm... uh... I've got it."

Her protests went unacknowledged.

And by the time Candice figured out what was happening she was on the sidewalk a few feet away from the building Jake was in, wondering how she had gotten herself into such as mess. She was a schoolteacher, not part of *The A-Team.* Her skills included getting a bunch of eleven-year-old brats to sit down and shut-up awhile, not this. A tough day on the job meant you had a fight with one of the other teachers, or a kid got hurt during recess, or one of the parents decided to give the school an unexpected visit because they were concerned with the way things were being run, after all, the school teachers were all idiots—why else would snot-nosed Danny be unable to wrap his head around both prime and composite numbers?

Candice pushed the palms of her hands into her eyes and when she was done she found that Dale was beside her. He smelled like rotten meat.

Kong's attention had been swayed elsewhere.

One of the men assisting her barked out a few words that she didn't quite catch before running to the far side of the street. He pulled a gun from behind his back and began firing. The other—a red haired man with a spray of blood across his white dress shirt—stayed with Candice, saying, "Are you alright? You hurt?"

"I'm okay," Candice responded, without considering the question. But in fact, she *was* okay. She had managed to run in and out of the war zone without getting herself killed, and that was practically a full-blown phenomenon.

"Dale?" she asked.

The red-haired man nodded. Dale was right there, less than three feet away.

"Is he alive?" Candice made her way to her husband. Dale's eyes were closed, his skin was pale; his body was covered in gore. He looked like he had been dragged up from the bottom of a swamp.

"I don't know," the man said.

"Help me pull him inside?" Candice asked.

After looking over his shoulder, the man reluctantly said, "Sure lady. I'll pull him inside but I can't stay. I've got—"

"That's okay. Just help me get him inside the door. I'll take it from there."

The man nodded, glad to be let off the hook.

KIRBY

Long before Kirby set foot on the property he knew there was nobody home. The driveway leading to the back-split home was empty, interior and exterior lights were off, and the front door was closed tight. If this wasn't enough, waiting to be picked up on the steps of the porch was a newspaper rolled into a loose, elastic-tied tube. These were all good signs.

He approached the house hiding a smile and excited about the near future. His original plan included knocking on the front door and assessing the situation from there, but his new plan, the one falling together uncontested, had him thinking the less time he spent standing in front of the house the better. Not that people were watching. Aside from a single family that were busy loading luggage into their car halfway down the street, the neighborhood appeared to be empty. The time to make a move was upon him.

The gate door, which led to the backyard, squeaked when he opened it but not enough to draw attention. He peeked through several windows before trying his luck with the side door, which was locked. No biggie. He figured it would be.

He listened. He knocked lightly. He listened some more. He knocked again, louder this time.

Nothing.

The house was empty. He was sure.

If the bitch owned a pet he was guessing cat, not dog.

Acting as if the house was *not* empty, Kirby pulled the key ring from his pocket and passed judgment on every key. Two of them were small, like they belonged to bicycle lock or a file cabinet. Two had the letters GM marked on each side, and were obviously for a car—probably the most expensive car *General Motors* had ever manufactured. Fucking bitch. One of the keys looked old and rustic, as if it was built for opening a locker or a trunk. Four of the keys appeared to be house keys.

He tried his luck. After three attempts he was in business and he stepped inside. The kitchen was clean, so was the living room and the dining room. "Hello?"

Nothing.

A little louder: "Hello?"

Still nothing. He was alone.

"Jesus, disease-us," he said, licking some of the moisture from his lips. The inside of his mouth was constantly filling with blood and fluid. The open wound he had earned earlier needed medical attention and would soon become infected. His face, in an uncompromising state of throbbing, hurt more than he wanted to admit. Thinking about the incident he said, "Bitch, you're in for a world of pain now. A *world* of pain!"

Standing in the front hall, away from the big living room windows, he spotted a family portrait on the wall—mother, son… and *father*. There was a *man* in the equation. Well, wasn't that special? Things might just get interesting for the family of assholes. Oh yes. Things might get very interesting indeed.

They won't be expecting a visitor when they arrive home. They won't be expecting anything at all, apart from another day of sunshine and happiness, until it's too late, which will be great... except...

A feeling came over him, one he didn't much care for.

Just *why*, exactly, did he have such a hard-on for this woman? Precisely, what had the woman done?

First of all, he scolded himself, *this isn't a woman—this is a corpse-fucker. A cold hearted corpse-fucker-bitch. There's a difference. She's no different than the corpse-fuckers in Athlete's Delight, and no different than the corpse-fuckers that treated me like shit back in high school. In fact, she might even be worse. Probably is worse, so don't start getting all soft. It's payback time.*

Yes, yes. But what did the "corpse-fucker" do that was so terrible?

She planted that spoon inside my face!

How do you like those tomatoes?

The war of words fell silent for a moment as Kirby stepped into the living room, investigating the knick-knacks on the shelves, the conservative-style furniture, the family photographs. He didn't like what he was seeing. The bitch considered herself the cat's meow. That much was obvious.

Yes, she attacked me, he thought, righteously.

She's the one—

But she did that *after*, right? She attacked *after* she was in danger.

That's not the point.

But it *is* the point. She didn't do anything wrong. She defended herself after she was in danger, but *WHY* was she in danger? What brought *that* on?

NO! That's NOT the point! It's in the way she looks at me, the way she mocks me, the way she judges me. She thinks she's so smart, so pretty, so perfect. A bitch like that has a way of making everyone feel a little smaller than they really are. She takes away confidence. She instills anxiety. She causes sadness, depression, and despair. A bitch like that has no place on this earth. The world would be a better place without her. And I want to make the world a better place. It's the right thing to do!

A rogue thought came, one that had him thinking about leaving both house and woman alone. *This isn't right,* he thought. *I'm not thinking straight,* he thought. But he pushed the objectionable considerations down into that dark place, that secret place, the place he forced all his unwanted thoughts to live. He wasn't going to leave the woman… *no, scratch that*… the *bitch* alone. Not after what she did. He was going to make her pay.

Yes, she would pay for the things she did. She would pay all that she owed and then some. He would make sure of it. His compensations would not be denied.

Far off but getting closer, he could hear the sound of Kong's roar. And somehow it made him feel better.

CANDICE

The red-haired man helped haul Dale inside the building. True to his word, he then left Candice to her own devices. This didn't upset Candice; she was grateful for the help and understood that he had problems of his own.

Just as the man was stepping outside Dale coughed and turned on his side, spitting god-knows-what from his mouth.

Candice, who had begun excepting that fact that Dale might already be dead, nearly screamed with delight.

"Dale! Dale!" she said, falling to her knees and pulling him close. "Dale! Oh my God, you're alive!"

Dale struggled to open his eyes, as if they had been pasted together with slow-bonding glue. They were red and swollen and layered with muck, shifting this way and that as he tried to make sense of his new surroundings. He was free of the beast, but not free of the nightmare.

"Help," he said, with short quick breaths. "Help me."

"I'm right here, baby." Candice responded, holding his head in her hands.

"Puffer... I... need my... puffer..."

At first Candice wasn't sure what Dale was saying. But then she knew, and realized just how frightened he had become.

Dale had a severe asthma condition that he kept under control by inhaling a drug called Fluticasone Propionate on a weekly basis. However, if he found himself in close proximity with certain animals his asthma would flare up and his lungs would close. If this happened he needed to inhale a drug called Terbutamol. Terbutamol relaxes the muscles in the airway making breathing easier. At one time Dale carried his Terbutamol inhaler everywhere. Then he realized that if he used Fluticasone Propionate more consistently the need for his Terbutamol inhaler became a rarity. The last time he needed the medicine he landed in the hospital for two days. That was three years ago.

Candice had almost forgotten about Dale's last trip to the emergency room, and how bad things had become. She thought she was going to lose him then, and she almost did. Thinking back, she could still see the look of terror claiming his eyes. His lungs were closed. He couldn't breathe…

"Oh shit," Candice said. "You're having a hard time breathing, aren't you?"

Eyes wide and worried, Dale shook his head. "My puffer… I need… my… puffer…"

For a second Candice didn't say anything, she didn't move. Dale needed to go to the hospital and he needed to go there immediately. He couldn't breathe. If she wasted too much time he would soon be dead, of this she had no doubt.

She closed her eyes and blocked out the sounds of the gunfire and the sirens, the screaming and the roars. She blocked out the madness that was playing out on the street and she put herself into a safe little box—a box built for two. Nothing else was important. Just her and Dale. She didn't have time to waste but she didn't have time to make mistakes either. Dale couldn't breathe, and the best way to deal with that would be what... what... what about Jake?

She left Jake upstairs.

Dale needed the hospital but Jake needed his mother.

She had to get Jake.

Eyes opening wide, she said, "Jake's..." Her voice disappeared for a moment and she needed to clear her throat before it returned. Her husband needed her, but her son did too. "Jake's upstairs. Stay right here and I'll be back in a minute with our son. Then the three of us can make our way to the hospital in no time."

Dale quickly considered, nodded, and tried to be strong, but the fear never left his face. It was rooted there, and the more his lungs closed the deeper those roots became. Dying was a real possibility.

Candice stood up. Looking down at her husband she wasted little time saying, "I love you, Dale. I'll be right back." Then she turned away and began running, leaving Dale alone and frightened as his lungs continued squeezing the life out of him. She ran up the stairs, past the fire extinguisher, and along the hall that was in serious need of repair. Slamming on the brakes she found herself standing in a hallway, wondering which door was the right one. All of the doors were closed now. Why were they closed? Was she on the wrong floor? Maybe. But wasn't this the right—?

"Damn!"

All at once she saw the note:

Mrs. Wanglund,

My name is Latina Havarti. I live in this apartment. Jake is with me on the first floor—apartment 199. Come right now. We will __not__ be there long.

Latina

"Shit!"

Candice read the note a second time, forcing the number 109 to stick in her head. Then she turned around and made her way along the hallway to the staircase, and down two flights of stairs.

It seemed that time was slipping away.

Jake was in apartment 109. Was that good news or bad? Did it matter? Maybe, maybe not. It probably didn't change things one way or another, unless...

She spotted 109 and opened the door without knocking. She raced inside and saw Jake talking with one woman while another woman was hanging up the phone.

"Mom!" Jake shouted, looking excited and more than a little relieved.

Candice acknowledged Jake with her eyes, then asked, "Do you guys have an inhaler? My husband has asthma and he needs an inhaler right now!"

A pause.

"Well, do you have one?!"

"I don't," Latina said.

Tobi shook her head. "No. Me neither."

"Shit! You don't know of anyone in the building that might have one?"

The answer was no.

Candice started to panic. What was she going to do? Dale needed to get to the hospital, but she didn't have a car. Well... actually, she did, but Kong had destroyed it earlier in the day. This left her with one clear-cut option—

"I need a car... do you guys have one?"

Things were moving too quickly for Latina and Tobi, who hadn't even been properly introduced to the woman standing before them, asking for an automobile. Tobi looked to Latina for guidance while she allowed a few mumbles and murmurs to slip past her lips. Latina's shoulders moved up an inch and her mouth opened and closed, but there were no words to accompany these actions.

This strummed an insufferable chord with Candice, who was becoming furious with both women. She didn't have time to watch them grope their succession of priorities; she only had time for answers. Distraught, she shouted, "Come on! My husband's dying!" She pointed at Jake. "Jake's father is dying! We need to get him to the hospital *right now!* I need a car!"

Latina said, "I've got a car, and we're just getting ready to leave. Do you want to come with us?"

That seemed like a workable solution, but before Candice had a chance to respond Tobi announced, "You can have mine." She turned, lifted her purse from the coffee table, and pulled a set of keys from it. She dropped her purse onto a chair and began separating car keys from her other keys, saying, "My car is a 2012, HHR. It's black, looks a little like a hearse. It's parked behind the building... you can't miss it."

Candice nodded gratefully, realizing for the first time that her own purse was long gone. She had lost it somewhere, but didn't know where. "Thank you," she said. "How do I get around back?"

"Did you come in the front door?"

"Yeah."

"Well, take the hallway the opposite direction. Again, you can't miss it." She handed a key to Candice, and then she said, "Before you go, two things. First, I have business cards in my glove box. My phone number is on them. Phone me when you're done so I can get my car back."

"Okay."

"And the hospital on George Street is gone. Kong knocked it down a little more than an hour ago."

"Are you sure?"

"I'm positive. I was there when it happened. You're going to have to go to the one—"

"The hospital in Whidbey," Candice said. It was a forty-minute drive if traffic wasn't too bad. She could probably do it in less than a half hour if she ignored stoplights and speed limits.

"Yes," Tobi confirmed. "The hospital in Whidbey."

"Okay. This key… it opens—?"

"It opens the door and starts the ignition. Now go."

"Thank you." Candice said, snagging Jake by the hand. "Come."

DALE

I would never say I wasn't afraid while I was inside Zombie Kong, but I will say the fear hit closer to home while I was lying on the floor inside the apartment building waiting for my wife to return. In some ways, being inside Kong was like suffering through a car accident: things happened so fast that the fear had no time to become entrenched. Lying on the hallway floor wasn't like that. It was more like treading water in the middle of the ocean: the danger wasn't immediate, but I couldn't tread forever. I had time to think about my future, time to worry, and time to be afraid. My lungs were definitely closing and soon enough they'd be closed. When that happened I would die. Of this I had no doubt.

My head became cloudy, my vision faded, and eventually I passed out. When my eyes opened again they were burning. My body was aching all over, my throat was raw, and my lungs felt like they were being squeezed in a vice. If pain was a liquid I was swimming in it. Candice, yelling something, was standing over me, forcing me to my feet. Jake was there too, crying and terrified. I tried to tell him things would be okay but the words failed to come. I loved him then, which is to say... at that moment, even though I was suffering, I realized *how much* I loved my son. I loved him with all my heart and I wished I could have made the situation better for him, but sadly, some things cannot be controlled.

I allowed myself to be escorted down the hallway, through a couple of doors, and into a parking lot. The sun seemed much too bright and the heat was frying us. My slimy body was loaded into the front seat of a car I had never seen before—it wasn't ours, but for some reason Candice had the keys. We had barely pulled out of the parking lot when she said, "St. George hospital is gone; we can't go there. That leaves us with the hospital in Whidbey. Do you want us to drive straight there or do you want to go home and get your inhaler?"

The St. George hospital was gone? What? What does she mean, gone? When did that happen? I tried to answer her question but I couldn't. My lungs wouldn't allow it.

She said, "Home? You want to go home?"

I nodded, not sure which option was best. I was starting to think it didn't matter. I could hardly breathe, and I could feel myself fading into oblivion.

"Okay, we'll go home," she said, rolling down her window. The stench wafting off me was enough to kill a hundred men. I was vaguely aware that Jake had also rolled down his window before locking himself beneath his seatbelt. The car would never smell the same.

I was trying to apologize for my appalling odor when Candice said, "Where is it, Dale? The inhaler, I mean. Is it in the bedroom? It's inside the nightstand beside the bed, isn't it? In that top drawer?"

Again I nodded. Sometimes having someone that knew all your dirty little secrets was fantastic. Candice knew what I needed and where to find it, which was good news for me, if she hurried.

She drove quickly. The roads weren't too bad considering the circumstances. When she pulled into our driveway she said, "I'm going to run in and out. I'll be back in two seconds. Just stay here!"

From the backseat, Jake said, "Do you want me to come with you, Mom? I sort of need to use the bathroom, anyhow."

"Stay with your father, Jake! I mean it. You can use the bathroom later."

As Jake's shoulders slumped Candice jumped out of the car and I managed to whisper, "Hurry." It was the last real word I would say. And as I looked down at my hands, consumed in fear, I noticed that color, as I had always known it, was becoming something different, something less vibrant. Perhaps I was going colorblind.

Or maybe, just maybe, I was about to die.

CANDICE

Before leaping from the car Candice reached across the seat for her purse, but then she remembered that she had lost it. Even though she felt no joy thinking about all the items she needed to replace, a lost purse, in view of the situation, was no big deal. There was a spare key hiding beneath a rock in the backyard, which she didn't use often, but on occasion it was a lifesaver.

She ran up the driveway and flung open the gate leading into the backyard. As she was racing past the side door she noticed that the inside door was open. *Why is it open?* she thought, but dismissed that line of thinking while skidding to a stop. She grabbed the exterior door-handle, swung the door open, and bolted into her home. Making excellent time she weaved through the house and into her bedroom. Within milliseconds she had the top drawer of the nightstand open and Dale's puffer in hand. Relief, delicate and frail, touched her briefly as she spun away from the nightstand. Things were going to be okay, she was almost sure of it.

Kirby was there, standing in the doorway with dried blood caked to his face. Once again his head was cocked in an outlandish, predatory manner. He wore a grin that reminded her of a sick cat.

"Hello Candice," he said with his chicken-eyes bolted to her and his smile growing wider all the time. "What do we have here?"

Candice screamed.

He's here... in the house. The maniac from the restaurant is inside the house! But how did he know where to look? And how does he know my name?

There were so many questions, too many questions, and all of them seemed to come pouring in at once.

He must have followed us home. Is that what happened? Maybe... but no, that didn't quite fit. If he followed us home there was no way he could have gotten inside the house so quickly. Not without running in after me. He didn't do that, did he? I didn't hear anything. I didn't hear him racing into the house, following me. He must have been inside already.

Of course. The door was unlocked.

He unlocked it, but how? How did he know which house was mine? How did he know I would come? How did he know which bedroom I would run into? Did he break a window? The door looked all right, didn't it? No broken frame; no hammer marks on the doorknob. Could he have found the key beneath the rock? How would he know where to look, unless...? Have we met before? Is that it, or is today the first time we've met? Maybe it wasn't. Maybe he has been watching me for months, or years. That would explain what happened in the restaurant, at least a little. Was this freak of nature a peeping Tom, upset for some unknown and illogical reason?

What about the front door? Did he come through the front door, and then unlock the side door later? That had potential; perhaps it was likely. I didn't waste one glance when it came to the front door, because I didn't have the key to the front door.

I lost the key—

He had the key. He had everything.

The key was in my purse and I left the purse in the restaurant. My wallet was in the purse, loaded with identification—driver's license, birth certificate, insurance information... who knows what else. Yes, of course. It all made sense. He unlocked the side door with my key, the one that was inside my purse. If only I had remembered to grab it before running out of the restaurant! If only—

"You're dead, corpse-fucker. Any questions?"

Candice released a groan.

She needed to escape, but Kirby was standing in the doorway. She glanced towards the window—curtains, blinds, and a ten-foot drop to the garden outside... at *least* a ten-foot drop. Maybe more. What was she going to do, jump through two sheets of glass? Unlikely. If she tried to be a Hollywood stuntman chances were she would break her neck, so what were her other choices?

Kirby was holding something in his hand—

A baseball bat.

Oh shit, he had Jake's baseball bat—the one Dale bought for Jake's birthday last summer. It was expensive, too, if she remembered correctly. Expensive things didn't break easily. They were durable, built to last. Especially when their only bona fide occupation was hitting things.

She was in trouble.

"You're scared," Kirby said. "I can see it in your eyes."

"What do you want? What are you doing here?"

Kirby took a step forward. His free hand was opening slowly and snapping shut. "I'll tell you what I'm doing here. I'm doing whatever the hell I want."

The psycho seemed to be more in tune now than before, Candice realized. She wasn't sure if this was good news or bad. The fact that his thinking was more coherent meant he would have the ability to be more devious, more cunning, but it also meant she would have a better chance of rationalizing with him. Maybe she could talk him down, make him understand that she wasn't the bad guy here. She didn't do anything wrong... aside from stabbing him in the face, that is.

She wondered if it was possible to have him see things her way.

Slim to none, she thought. *My odds are slim to none, and Slim left town.*

Any questions?

Is that what he said? *Any questions?* What kind of bug-shit inquiry was that? She wanted to throw something at him and make it count, but the only thing in her hand was Dale's inhaler and she didn't want to throw *that.* Dale needed it. In fact, now that she thought about it, she didn't have time for this... *any* of this. Dale was waiting.

She needed to do something, but what?

There was a clock on the dresser, ticking away irrelevantly. Maybe she could reach out and grab it before the psycho knocked her block off. It wasn't much of a plan, but it was the only one she had coming to her.

Stepping towards the dresser she switched the inhaler from her right hand to her left. She swallowed back her fears and leaned in.

Kirby said, "When I was child—"

Terror pushed into her, making Candice nervous. She stepped back, afraid to do anything but listen to his voice.

"—I had a baseball bat," Kirby continued, his chicken-eyes narrowing. "It wasn't as nice as this one. It was old and dirty and very well loved. I gave it a name: *Smasher.* I used Smasher a lot. Mostly, I'd use it to go suckerfishin' down at Cooper's creek with a boy named David Camions. David was a mean little bastard that liked fighting kids that were smaller than him... when he got a little older he was in and out of jail more times than I can recall, which everyone expected. But a few years ago I ran into David and we got talking about the good old days, back before jail, in those long days when we'd spend the summertime fishin'. He changed his name, David did... he was calling himself Elmer Wright, if I remember correctly. Anyways, David—*Elmer*, if you prefer—he'd hold the net and I'd swing the bat. We had it down to a science. Do you know what suckerfish are?"

Candice shook her head, whispering, "No."

"Suckerfish are about a foot long and they have these big Mick Jagger lips. If it weren't for the lips they'd kind of look like a trout or a bass, but you can't eat 'em. Don't ask me why. Fish are put on this earth for one reason and one reason only... to eat. And if you can't eat 'em, do you know what they're good for? *Nothing*." Kirby brought the bat up and sat it on his shoulder. His free hand continued opening slowly and snapping shut. "We'd go down to Cooper's creek with David's net and my old bat and hunt suckerfish. I'd club 'em and David would scoop 'em up. Then we'd lay 'em on a rock and beat the shit out of 'em. Sometimes, if you hit 'em in the right spot—the *sweet spot*—their guts would squeeze out of their mouths like toothpaste from the tube. When we were finished we'd toss what was left of the bastards back in the creek. It was friggin' awesome."

Thumb between her teeth, Candice started thinking about that window again. Maybe she could jump through it after all. Or maybe she could charge full steam ahead and knock the psycho on his ass before he knew what was happening. Yeah. That was a better plan. Maybe she could do that.

"Anyways," Kirby said, still grinning, "I figure this bedroom here makes a pretty good net, and this bat may not be Smasher, but I think it'll do the job just fine. I'm going to beat the shit out of you, bitch. I'm gonna hit you right in the sweet spot, and when I'm finished I'm gonna throw your remains in the creek."

Kirby's chicken-eyes widened as he tightened his grip and lifted the bat from his shoulder.

And that's when Candice charged him.

JAKE

Locked in his seatbelt, ignoring the terrible smell that was radiating from his father, Jake flinched at the unexpected sounds coming from behind him. When he spun around he saw Kong standing between two bungalows, intestines hanging to his feet, slamming fists against both houses. One of the houses was hanging tough and taking the beating like a champ, the other... not so much; it was making a quick transition from home to scrap-heap. With the monster turned the opposite direction, fighting a battle with the citizens from one street over, Jake couldn't see the look of fury on Kong's face but it was certainly there. Cutting through neighborhoods, oblivious to the fact that people's yards weren't considered a throughway for traffic, was doing nothing for the beast's disposition. He was angrier than a nest of wasps getting swatted by a stick. Jake couldn't help wondering where Kong would go next, and how safe he was sitting in a borrowed car a few hundred feet away.

After watching the battle for nearly two minutes three cars came racing down the street. All three cars parked in unusual angles on the street between Jake and Kong, creating an unintentional roadblock for oncoming traffic. Jake counted six men jumping out of the three cars—every one of them armed. They opened fire on the beast without hesitation.

After being shot several times Kong spun around and rushed the nearest car. He slammed a foot on top of it, destroying the front end. Men scattered like roaches.

This startled Jake, making him appreciate the fact that he wasn't watching some new form of entertainment, but the real thing. He was in a dangerous place, a place he would be smart to get away from, a place that was getting more and more dangerous all the time.

He turned away from the chaos and shouted, "Dad! Dad! We've got to get out of here! Dad!" He unbuckled his seatbelt, slid forward, and grabbed his father by the shoulder. "Dad!"

Dale wasn't moving.

"Dad—?"

Jake pulled his hand away as if he had touched something foul, and he inched his way back into his seat. He looked at his hand and then looked at his father once again. *What's happening here? Why isn't Dad responding?* Jake opened the car door and stepped outside slowly, like a boy that didn't want to know what would transpire next. Almost cautiously he looked at his father through the passenger door window. The window—still rolled up—was clean, allowing Jake a crystal clear view of something he didn't want to see. Dale's eyes were open but there was nobody home. The man was dead, and if he wasn't dead he looked dead. His chest wasn't moving, his head was skewed to one side, and his bottom lip was hanging away from the rest of his mouth in a way Jake had never seen before. He almost looked plastic, sitting frozen in place like a human replica in a wax museum.

"Oh no—" Jake said, as the reality of the moment came crashing in. Before Kong arrived his father was moving around quite a bit, struggling to breathe, trying to find a position that allowed a greater amount of air into his lungs. Now he was motionless—a silent and stagnant object, a piece of meat.

Things were bad. No, not *bad*. They were *so* bad... so terribly *wrong* for *so* many reasons. How long had he been sitting in the car with a corpse?

Jake leaned his forehead against the window and stood still for a long moment, his eyes heavy and emergent with tears.

What's taking Mom so long?

Suddenly he needed his mother. Yes... his mother. That was a good plan. Mom would know what to do, and maybe Dad wasn't even dead. Maybe he just *looked* dead. Maybe he could be fixed.

Kong roared as Jake ran across the yard to the front door. He was surprised to find the door locked. *Mom went through the other door,* he thought. Then he re-membered her opening the gate and running into the backyard. Like a man on a mission he bolted across the yard a second time. He pushed open the gate door, which had swung shut on its own, and zipped into the house through the side door.

"Mom!" he shouted. "Mom, come quick!"

And that's when he saw the man from the restau-rant, covered in blood, holding a baseball bat in his hand. The man grinned, and his little chicken-eyes seemed to dig holes right into Jake's heart.

DALE

When I woke-up things were different: the air had no smell, I was afraid of nothing, and more importantly, the aches and pains in my body were gone. I can't say breathing was easier, but I can say it was no longer an issue.

My lungs were no longer an issue.

There was no color in my world; everything had turned black, white, and gray. Sounds were muffled, like I was wearing earmuffs over ears packed with cotton. I could still hear things but sound seemed far away and irrelevant.

I looked at my hands. They were dirty and covered in a strange, jelly-like filth. I couldn't remember why, and I tried to say so but all that escaped my mouth was a mumble.

For a moment I didn't know what to do, but then I realized where I was: sitting in a car in front of my home. Instinctively, I fumbled with the car door until I managed to open it, and then I stepped outside. To my right was my home. To my left was a giant gorilla, engulfed in a battle with people I could no longer relate with. Why were the people fighting this poor, defenseless gorilla?

I looked the gorilla in the eye, and for a moment the gorilla looked at me.

The world seemed to stop then; everything became unnaturally quiet.

The two of us, gorilla and man, we both realized that we were connected somehow; we were the same. And because of this strange unity I knew, deep in my heart, that this giant beast would never hurt me, and I would never hurt it. We were brethren; we were family. We were special.

Our moment of tranquility came to an abrupt end with an onslaught on gunfire.

In my mind I told the beast that he should try to get away from the bad men, and that he was welcome to be with me.

In my mind he thanked me.

I turned away from the battle and shuffled my way towards the front door. Upon my arrival I discovered it was locked. After a moment I remembered that my home had more than one door. I made my way to the side of my house and opened the side door. I stepped inside.

Something was going on, something I couldn't understand.

It was bad. Whatever was happening, it was bad.

I took me a moment to maneuver myself into the living room. Walking was difficult.

There was a man standing in the center of the room. My wife was behind him in a wash of blood, smashed apart like an egg yolk and its shell. My son was lying at the man's feet. His head was splintered apart; the blood was rolling out of him, as if his head had been opened up the moment before.

In my mind I asked for help, because I didn't know what to do. My wife and my son were dead, murdered by the man standing before me. I didn't know who the man was, or why he had done such a thing to my family. All I knew for sure was that it wasn't right, and I needed to make things better somehow.

I looked at my wife; her chest was still moving. Even though her arms were broken, and her legs were broken, and her ribs had been smashed in, she was still alive. Somehow, she hadn't slipped away just yet.

I looked at my boy, and I watched as his eyes shifted position. He was looking up at me, pleading, begging. His head was split wide and the blood was bucketing out of him; his *life* was leaving him, but it hadn't left him yet. Soon, but not yet—

I didn't feel anything.

Feelings, much like color and sound, had faded from me. I knew the man was a bad man, and I knew that I should be angry with him. My wife and child were in pain; they were dying. This should have made me feel a lot of things but it didn't. I felt nothing.

The man was suddenly terrified. He started screaming something terrible about me; he clearly didn't like the way I looked. He ran to the front door, unlocked it, and bolted onto the street.

Through the living room window I could see the giant gorilla focus on the man, ignoring everything else. Somehow the great beast knew the man was my enemy, and thus, the man was *his* enemy. I turned away from the window just as the beast lowered a massive foot, killing for vengeance.

My wife and son were still alive, but not for long. Not without God.

Growing up, I never believed in God. But now I do.

So I dropped to my knees, not to pray, but to eat. And when I was on my hands and knees, eating my wife and son, I knew God was with me, guiding me, inviting my family to join in his everlasting glory.

Praise God, for He is the resurrection.

He brings us eternal life.

JAMES ROY DALEY is a writer, editor, and musician. He studied film at the Toronto Film School, music at Humber College, and English at the University of Toronto. He is the author of *Terror Town, Into Hell, 13 Drops of Blood,* and *The Dead Parade.* In 2009 he founded *Books of the Dead Press,* where he enjoyed immediate success working with many of the biggest names in horror. He edited anthologies such as *Zombie Kong - Anthology, Best New Vampire Tales, Classic Vampire Tales,* and *Best New Zombie Tales.*

Great titles from:
BOOKS OF THE DEAD

BEST NEW ZOMBIE TALES (Vol. 1)

BEST NEW ZOMBIE TALES (Vol. 2)

BEST NEW ZOMBIE TALES (Vol. 3)

BEST NEW ZOMBIE TALES TRILOGY

BEST NEW WEREWOLF TALES (VOL. 1)

BEST NEW VAMPIRE TALES (Vol. 1)

CLASSIC VAMPIRE TALES

GARY BRANDNER - THE HOWLING

GARY BRANDNER - THE HOWLING II

GARY BRANDNER - THE HOWLING III

GARY BRANDNER - THE HOWLING TRILOGY

JAMES ROY DALEY - INTO HELL

JAMES ROY DALEY - TERROR TOWN

JAMES ROY DALEY - 13 DROPS OF BLOOD

JAMES ROY DALEY - THE DEAD PARADE

JAMES ROY DALEY - ZOMBIE KONG

TONIA BROWN - BADASS ZOMBIE ROAD TRIP

MATT HULTS - ANYTHING CAN BE DANGEROUS

JOHN F.D. TAFF - LITTLE DEATHS

MATT HULTS - HUSK

TIM LEBBON - BERSERK

PAUL KANE - PAIN CAGES

ZOMBIE KONG ANTHOLOGY